The Bad Boy's

Pregnant

Bride

I0638408

Alyse Zaftig

ISBN: 978-1634810418

Alarm

Chris

My alarm went off, and I opened one eye. I had a girl wrapped in my arms. Fuck if I knew her name. She had long blonde hair, which looked hot, but it also was in my mouth. Ew. I spat it out. I was late to the graduation ceremony.

"You gotta go, babe."

She opened her eyes, turned, and reached for me, but I dodged her hands neatly.

"Get out. I've got somewhere to be."

She stuck out her lower lip. "But I thought we could have a repeat of last night."

"I don't have time, babe." I pulled her to the side of the bed, then I slapped her ass. "Good time last night." We'd stayed up past dawn getting to know one another.

She put her hand on my cheek and leaned in for a kiss, but I slid away from her. I didn't do sloppy seconds. It made girls want more than I really wanted to give.

"Leave."

I watched her sashay away from me. I knew that I wasn't going to fuck her again, but it was still a nice show. She tossed her hair over her shoulder and struck a pose.

"You sure?"

I nodded. "I'm late already." I watched as she found her dress and put it on.

"You left your bra."

"Keep it." She winked at me. "It's a souvenir." Her panties were nowhere to be seen, and she put on her heels very quickly and calmly, as if she woke in a stranger's bed every morning. She probably did.

"Bye, Chris."

I blinked. How did she know my name? I didn't remember much of last night. One, alcohol. Two, all the nights, clubs, and women ran together into a blur.

"What's your name?"

"Jordana." She winked at me again, and then she flounced out the door.

I headed into my shower to get her scent off of me. She smelled fine to me last night, but this morning, I wanted to scrape her sickly sweet scent off of my skin. Was there such a thing as whiskey goggles for your nose?

I turned on the shower and scrubbed everywhere. I should've been at my parents' house already to ride with them to Laila and Trouble's graduation. I'd text them to tell them that I was on my way.

I got dressed in one of my suits. When I was wearing one, I looked like a corporate drone, the son of a billionaire. Naked, I looked pretty different. It might have been the tats or the muscles honed from years of swimming, but girls loved to see me naked. I winked at myself in the mirror.

I combed my hair and used a little gel, and then I was ready to go.

My motorcycle wasn't a good choice when wearing a $5,000 bespoke suit. I felt edgy, though, even though I'd fucked Jordana's brains out last night.

I hopped into my little Lambo, a high school graduation gift from my parents, and headed towards USC's graduation ceremony. They were so insanely long and boring, but I figured that I owed them. Plus, my

dad was paying for the best

restaurant in town, one of Laila's

favorites, and I didn't want to miss

that.

Champagne and Jack

Chris

I slept through the boring graduation, then Trouble proposed to Laila and all of us went to Vegas for their wedding.

After the wedding, Trouble and Laila were basically on top of each other. Our parents had said goodbye to us after the brief ceremony — and Mrs. King had gotten a DVD of the whole thing — so the four of us went to a club to celebrate. We had Moet and Dom Perignon to celebrate that Trouble and Laila were married. From the way that they looked at each other, I knew that Nora and I were just cramping their style.

"For Pete's sake, guys. Get a room. I don't want to see you touching my sister."

The two of them turned to me, and Trouble's hand was on Laila's backside. He didn't seem concerned about it at all. "Yeah, dude, thanks for coming to my wedding."

He pulled Laila into his arms. She giggled as he pulled her off and said something about having his way with her.

Gross.

I tried to avoid thinking about my best friend being married to my little sister. Nora and I were still in a VIP booth with two magnums of champagne.

I drank it. It was sweet and light, but it didn't make my thoughts go away.

"Why don't we try something a little harder? How do you feel about Jack Daniels?"

Nora's eyes lit up. "Down for it."

I got someone's attention, and I got a little Jack at the table. I drank two shots immediately.

"I don't understand how my best friend could marry Laila. I know that they've been dating for a couple years, but he's young. Why would anybody date at this age?"

"They are in love. Aren't you happy for them?"

"I'd be happier for them if they weren't married to each other. Laila should've found someone her own age. Frankly, I'm glad that she didn't get an STD from Trouble."

Nora laughed a nice, light laugh. It was pretty. She was pretty. The lights were dim, but they caught on her earrings. Sparkly.

"I'm happy that they're together, and you should be, too."

"Well, I guess that I don't have to chase anybody off, so that's good. That's up to Trouble now." I did another shot of Jack.

"Think about it. There are plenty of benefits of being married. You have someone who is always there for you. And you can get down to baby-making when you're married. You go to sleep and wake up in the same bed as someone else, so it's pretty easy.

It's not as hard as picking up somebody in a bar."

I snorted. "Like it's hard for you to pick up somebody in a bar." I waved my hand over her. "You've got great tits."

She gasped. "Chris!"

"What?" I shrugged. "It's true. You do."

"You're not supposed to say that."

Her cheeks got a little red, and I just grinned. "I'd have to be dead not to notice your body, sweetheart." I drank another shot of Jack, and my body was feeling pleasantly loose.

"You should know. You've been picking up girls left and right since you went through puberty."

I lifted one shoulder and dropped it. "Sure, but it's getting boring, you know? I mean, yeah, it's nice to get some novelty, but it's too much work for one night. I'm thinking about getting a girlfriend, but I'm not sure how to get one of those."

I looked at Nora in the dim light. She was pretty. Drunk logic had me asking, "Would you like to date me?"

Nora shook her head. "No. You're a player."

I put a hand over my heart and pretended to be offended. "The nerve!" I burst out laughing a little too loudly, if the looks that I got from the table next to us were any indication. "I wouldn't play you, Nora."

"The only way that I'd trust a boy like you would be if you put your money where your mouth was. I'd love to see you married to some chick...that'd be quite an experience for her and you."

I thought about it. "Married. I'm not sure why anybody gets married."

"The sex, of course."

"You can get free-range sex when you want it, if you want it." I shook my head. "Marriage is forever."

"It doesn't have to be."

I shut my big mouth. I knew that Nora's mom had run off when she was a little kid, leaving her dad to raise her solo.

"It's forever for me. Maybe I'll get married in my 50s or 60s."

"And that's why you can't date me. I'm only looking for serious boys right now."

"Seriously? You've been with what, a dozen guys? Two dozen?"

She slurred as she told me, "I haven't been with any guys."

I snorted. "Whatever. During high school, I saw you with a new guy every week."

"I haven't ever had sex."

What? She hadn't ever had sex? I tried to count the number of partners I had had, and I lost count. My body was still in good shape, even after I left behind competitive swimming, and the ladies liked it.

"You're a virgin?" I looked her up and down. "You sure don't look like one." She had the kind of curves that guaranteed a good night and a secretive smile that made me sweat.

"It's a secret that even Laila doesn't know."

She put her finger on my lips. "And you can't tell anybody."

I took her finger and bit it lightly. I pulled her into my lap, and I bent her back movie-star style as I thrust my tongue into her mouth. She participated, grinding on me and making my pants a little too tight. I smelled her fresh scent, and I knew that I needed her desperately.

"You're sure that I can't convince you to come to my room tonight?"

"Only if we get married," she giggled.

I threw back another shot. I had

reasons why I didn't want to be

married, but I was having a hard time

remembering them. Why not? "Right.

We're getting married." Maybe it was

the alcohol, but I felt a rush of

warmth fill my body.

Wedding Chapel

Nora

"Woohoo! I'm going to the chapel and I'm gonna get maaaarried!"

Chris took my arm. "Don't fall over. You're wearing pretty tall heels."

In my drunken haze, I considered it. On one hand, having heels on meant that Chris would stay connected to me. On the other, being heavily inebriated while wearing stilettos would end in tears.

"Hold on, buddy. Gotta take off my shoes."

I used his arm for support while I took off my heels. I was barefoot, and I didn't care.

"Much better."

"Are you sure you want to get married?"

"Sure, why not? I've got nothing better to do." I jumped on Chris, and he caught me just in time. I planted a loud, smacking kiss on his mouth.

"Gonna be married to the hottest guy around."

I slid down his body, forcing him to let me go. "And you know that it's all about the wedding night."

"Mmm..." Chris said as he kissed me again and again. "I'll like that."

Neither of us was very sober when we walked into the chapel. In no time at all, we'd gotten married by Elvis with two gold wedding bands and a small diamond ring that the chapel sold us, signed things, and had a marriage certificate that said

that we were Mr. and Mrs.
Christopher King.

We walked outside, and the fresh air hit me like a drug.

"Honeymoon sex!" I yelled. "We're going to have honeymoon sex!" Nobody stared. It was Vegas after all.

Chris held me up, but he wasn't walking straight either. We made our way back into a taxi.

While we were in the taxi, I reached under my dress and shimmied out of my lace thong.

"Here, husband. You can have this."

I put it into the inner pocket of his jacket. I kissed him on the mouth.

Suddenly, a thought occurred to me. I spun and saw the cab driver looking at us in the rearview mirror. I realized that public sex in a cab probably wouldn't be a good idea.

I put my hand on his knee and whispered in his ear, "I can't wait to get you into a real bed."

He leaned me back and bit me hard on my neck. I moaned and

arched my back, feeling fire spread from where he bit me. He whispered back, "That's for making me wait."

Chris paid the driver, and we went upstairs to his hotel room. He had a nicer room than mine. I'd gotten a junior executive suite, which had a little living room, desk, and a bedroom with a little bathroom.

He had some kind of ultra-executive suite or something. He had a gigantic king bed, a kitchen, a living room, and a huge bathroom. It had a Jacuzzi.

"It's so hot in Vegas," I told Chris. "I think I'd like to wash off."

I unzipped my dress, and I let it fall to the floor. His eyes almost popped out of his head.

"Holy mother of..."

I turned on the tap, bending over so he could see the curve of my butt. He came to stand behind me, and he rubbed it a little bit.

"Is this okay?" he asked. "I want to make sure."

"We're married," I told him. "Of course you can touch. Now get naked and into the tub."

He took off his clothes faster than most drunk people could. Heck, it was probably faster than most sober people could.

He got into the tub and reached for me.

Jacuzzi

Chris

I pulled Nora into my lap and pulled her in for a deep kiss. She rolled her hips on me like a pro, and I pinched her nipple. She squeaked a little, then she moaned as I broke her kiss and started biting her neck hard. I couldn't go down on her in the Jacuzzi, so I brought my hand between her legs and thrust two fingers inside. I could feel her muscles clench around them, and I knew that she was ready.

"I want your hands on the side of the tub. Don't move them."

She shot her hands on either side of me, and I guided my cock into her wet slit.

We moaned at the contact. Her eyes were closed tightly, but mine were open. I wouldn't miss a minute of this. She was breathing hard, and I was going to make her pant.

I slid a hand towards her sacrum and rubbed it while guiding her up and down on my cock. The warm water was splashing everywhere, but I didn't care. I felt fire shoot inside of me, and I knew that it wouldn't be very long before I couldn't hold on anymore.

Her hips kept the hard rhythm as I let go of her, and I put my hand between us to flick her clit. Her whole body shuddered, her breasts moving, as she screamed while she orgasmed.

I finally closed my eyes as I shot inside of her.

Seconds past. They might have been minutes. Or hours. I wasn't sure. I was in the warm water with Nora in my lap, her head on my shoulder. I had my arms wrapped around her, stroking her back slowly.

"I want to fuck you on the bed," I told her. "Let's get out of the Jacuzzi."

I stood up with her on my arms. We dripped water everywhere. When we got to the bedroom, I threw her facedown at the edge of the bed, her feet on the ground, but her stomach on the bedspread.

"Don't move an inch," I commanded. I grabbed a the tie from the suit I'd worn to the graduation dinner. I tied her securely. I hadn't been in Boy Scouts for long, but I knew how to tie more than just a granny knot.

"Try to pull your hands apart." She tried, but she couldn't. The bonds would hold.

"Perfect."

I spread her pussy lips apart so that I could spear her with my tongue. I felt the shock race through her body, and then she melted slowly like a popsicle left in the sun.

She tasted better than a popsicle, all spice and sugar. My hand stimulated her clit while my tongue lapped up her juice, and she quivered through two orgasms before she spoke again. Well, recognizable words, anyway.

"Please."

I took my tongue out of her. "Please what?"

"Please take me."

"I thought you'd never ask." I smacked her ass, leaving a red handprint on one side. Then I was guiding my cock inside of her, and she was shouting again.

And so was I.

I wrapped my hand around her throat, pushing her up and down on my cock. I wasn't hurting or choking her, but I had to admit that I liked to have that control.

I sped up the rhythm, making sure to angle myself so that her clit was rubbed by the bedspread. As her muscles started fluttering, I groaned. She milked everything out of me, every drop that I had inside. I filled her again and again, even after I was done. I was still hard.

I got on the bed and spooned her from behind, still inside of her. My arm went around her luscious hip and rested between her thighs. I bit her ear and kissed her neck.

"Did you like your honeymoon sex, Mrs. King?"

"Very much, Mr. King." She turned her head, and I lifted myself a little bit to kiss her. It was funny, because we'd just done the wild thing, but this kiss tasted like a first kiss. It was soft. Sweet. Gentle.

I was none of those things, so I took control again by taking my hands away from her juicy thighs and pinching a nipple.

"Ouch!"

I liked to mix pain and pleasure. I pinched the other one a little softer, and she threw her head back a little.

I could take her again. This time, I rolled us so that she was completely facedown on the bed. Her hands were still tied together, so she couldn't do much. I bent her so that her knees were underneath her stomach, then I bit her shoulder and rode her.

I pulled her hair, forcing her to arch her back. She was breathing heavily when she came apart beneath me. I knew how to hit her G-spot, and

I put my hand around her front to touch her clit again.

I controlled the movement of her pelvis as I crashed inside of her again and again. I felt my balls draw up a split second before I filled Nora with my seed. This time, it came in slower spurts. I held her absolutely still until I was done.

I pulled out of her, and I rolled her over. I put my arm around her shoulder, and I held her face against my chest. I kissed her forehead.

"You like it like that? A little rough, a little pain, but so much pleasure."

"Yeah." Her voice was sleepy, and I closed my eyes. There'd be time for another round in the morning. I fell asleep with Nora in my arms.

Waking Up in Vegas

Nora

I opened one eye. I was warm. Too warm. My head hurt like I had a hangover. I was a little sweaty. I guessed that I had bundled up too thoroughly in my blankets last night.

I was abruptly conscious that there was something hard and warm against my back.

I smelled something, and I started sweating for another reason. There was somebody in bed with me.

Despite my wild-child ways, I didn't sleep in other people's beds. I'd never had a morning after. My heart was hammering out of my chest when I looked over my shoulder.

My heart rate skyrocketed as I realized who it was: Chris King.

Oh no.

Without bothering to be quiet, I unbundled myself from the sheets. There was no way to extricate myself without waking him up, and I wasn't even going to try. I needed my clothes and purse, and then I'd be able to get out.

Chris was a deep sleeper, because all the commotion didn't wake him up. I got dressed in last night's clothes. I looked at the remains of my shredded panties, and I tucked them into my purse. No sense in just leaving them here.

I put on my shoes, looked in the mirror, shuddered from how hideous I was, hair a total mess, and then

went to my own room, just a few
doors down in the hotel.

I got inside and took off my
dress. I looked at myself in the full-
length mirror. I had some bite marks
on my skin, and I traced them lightly.
They didn't hurt. They only served as
reminders of all the passion that I'd
felt last night.

I sniffed, and I knew that I still
smelled like him. I felt sticky between
my thighs.

Time for a shower.

I went over to my shower, and I took off everything. Last night was a mistake, a huge one. I'd finally succumbed to Chris King's charms. I'd wondered about them for years, of course, but now I had the bite marks to remember him by.

I didn't mean to get tangled up with Chris King. I'd watched him change girls more often than he changed clothes, and I didn't want to get involved with that.

I knew that Jordana had tried to run game on Chris King. She had tried to force him to settle down with her, telling him that she was pregnant right after they'd had sex. It was ridiculous. She had tried really hard to catch him in the baby trap, but nobody had believed her. In a shocking twist, in the subsequent months, she claimed that she had a miscarriage. Jordana had disappeared for a while. There were rumors that she had moved to Canada, but nobody knew exactly where she was. Chris had dodged a bullet with that one.

As I turned and felt the ache between my legs, I thought about telling Laila that I'd been with her brother. I should probably give it a lot of time...she was still in the happy honeymoon phase with Trouble, and she would be shocked by me hooking up with her older brother. She knew that I had a thing for him, but I had never acted on it.

And now I had. I was smarter than getting involved with Chris. I figured that it would be a one-time thing...our secret. It wasn't as if Chris trumpeted whom he'd been with, especially since it changed so fast. He was very quick to let girls go.

I didn't know why I was worrying about all of this. It was a one-night stand.

That's when I noticed that there was a sparkly princess-cut diamond on my ring finger.

Waking Up Alone

Chris

I woke up in bed with my cock aching and leaking a little bit. I could smell the scent of a woman in my sheets, and I rolled over to grasp her tightly around the waist.

But I gripped empty air.

I opened my eyes. I was alone in the bed. I sat up. My door was closed, and my clothes were nowhere to be seen.

Where was I?

I looked around and saw how sterile everything was. Right. Hotel room.

Yesterday came back. Trouble and Laila had decided to get married, and I...

I looked down at my hand, and I saw my gold wedding band.

Oh shit.

I looked at myself in the mirror. I looked like hell. My head throbbed, and I needed some coffee stat.

I lifted the telephone, and I called the concierge.

"I'd like eggs, bacon, and coffee for breakfast, please."

"We'll have that up to your room in 30 minutes, sir."

"Thank you."

I hung up my phone and went to the shower.

I went to the Jacuzzi, and I frowned. I apparently hadn't drained it last night and it seemed a little

pink. Did the hotel have pink mold?

Reality slapped me in the face. I

remembered surging into a female

body while I took her hard.

Had I hurt anybody? I was very,

very careful to get consent

beforehand.

I got completely still as

realization washed over me. I'd had a

virgin last night.

I didn't have many rules, but

absolute honesty was one of them. A

virgin had no place in my bed.

I stared at my wedding band as if it were an alien.

Why was I married? Was this a practical joke?

I took a shower, and I felt a little more human afterwards. I brushed my teeth, and then I got dressed. A guy on the hotel staff knocked on my door and brought in my breakfast. I tipped him and closed the door behind him.

I ate my eggs. The bacon tasted crispy, and I regretted not asking for toast to eat with my eggs. Next time.

I drank coffee, and then I was finally awake.

I saw a piece of paper on the table near the door.

It was a marriage certificate. Why had I taken Laila and Trouble's marriage certificate home?

A cold ball of fear and dread settled in my stomach as I read it. It had my name on it.

I was married.

To Nora.

Finding Nora

Chris

I went to my chair and sat down hard. I had no idea how I ended up married.

I did the math. Vegas. A lot to drink. Did that equal the marriage certificate in my hand?

I needed to talk to Nora.

I walked down the hallway, and I saw that her door was open. There was a housekeeping cart next to it.

I walked into her hotel room, but it was spotless.

"Hi," I told the maid, who was staring at me. I pulled a $20 out of my pocket. "Here's a tip. I was wondering if you could tell me where the occupant is?"

She shook her head.

I switched to Spanish. "Where is the occupant?"

"She's gone. I got the order to clean up this room two hours ago. That's all I got."

I tipped the maid the $20 bill, and then I walked out and went back to my own room. Nora had run this morning.

I sighed. My sister probably had Nora's number, but the morning after her wedding probably wasn't the best time to contact her.

To be strictly honest, it was the morning after my wedding, too.

I started packing up my stuff in my hotel room. I didn't have much, since I wasn't expecting to hit Vegas. I had my suit and a change of clothes that I'd bought quickly yesterday.

My phone rang.

"Are you ready to leave?" That was my dad. Pretty direct.

I looked around my room. "Yeah. I'll meet you in the lobby in 2 minutes."

I picked up my stuff, went to the hallway, closed my door, and headed towards the elevators.

They were very fast, and I was in the lobby in no time.

My parents were standing there.

"Hey, slugger." My dad clapped me on the back. "Are you ready to go back to LA?"

"Yeah. So, what, are we just ditching Laila and Trouble here? What about Nora?"

"No, we'll send the plane back for them. Mr. McKane needs to get back to work, and so do I. Instead of making his jet come out here, we figured that we'd hitch a ride with Allen."

"Allen?"

"Yes, I guess we're on first-name terms with Trouble's dad." My dad shrugged. "Let's get going, kid."

The three of us walked straight out in the pure, searing heat of Las Vegas. It was so dry here that I could practically feel my skin crack.

My mom had already called a limo, and it took us to the private hangar of the Vegas airport. Mr. McKane — I was never going to think of him as "Allen" — was sitting there with his laptop. He waved when we got in but didn't make conversation.

As soon as I sat in my soft leather seat, I yawned. I guessed that I hadn't slept much last night. I heard the gentle thrum of the engines as we taxied. As we took off, I went out like a light.

* * *

When I woke up, I texted Nora. No response. I nudged a private investigator I used sometimes, and I gave him her number.

He got back to me a few hours later to say that he couldn't trace the phone at all. He said that she probably was keeping it in a Faraday cage.

It looked like I would need to wait for Nora to get back to me. I was not a patient man, and I'd look for her, even if my PI thought that it was hopeless.

Porcelain

Nora

THREE MONTHS LATER

I woke up for the fourth day to immediately worship the porcelain god.

I was on my knees next to the toilet, and I felt my tears start to fall. They splashed softly on the cream tile of my bathroom. I knew what it meant. I couldn't lie to myself that I had a stomach bug. I knew what had happened.

Yesterday, it had crossed my mind that Chris and I hadn't used protection when we were together that night. I was a coward.

Laila had given him my number, but she told me that she didn't want to get between the two of us.

I hadn't been answering any of his texts or calls. It looked like I would need to.

I stood up and washed my mouth out with a little mint Listerine. I went back to my bedroom to pick up my iPhone, which was charging on my nightstand.

I looked at my missed calls and called Chris.

The phone was picked up on the first ring.

"Hello?"

"Hi, Chris."

"Nora, where have you been?"

"I want to meet you."

"So do I. Why else would I be calling you?"

"Are you free tonight?"

"Yeah, I'm free anytime you want to talk about our marriage."

Marriage. The concept made my blood turn to ice. Who knew that marriage would even happen for me? I had planned to be single forever, but I'd gotten married in Vegas. I shook my head at drunk Nora.

"There's a diner where we can talk. I'll see you in an hour. Do you have a pen?"

"Give me a minute."

"You know what? I'll text it to you instead."

I pulled the phone away from my ear, and I texted him the address.

I didn't realize until I hung up the phone that I was crying. Not gentle, delicate lady-like tears. I was sobbing, and he'd probably heard it while I was on the phone.

What was I going to do? If I had wanted to abort the baby, I wouldn't have told Chris, but calling him was my first instinct. I knew that if I had a baby, I wanted him to be part of the child's life.

What would Laila think? She definitely knew that something was going on between me and her brother, but she also didn't want to get involved...but she would be if she had a niece or nephew cooking.

I threw some cold water on my face. I didn't want my eyes to look red when I met Chris.

I got dressed to meet Chris in the diner. Normally, I wore a little makeup. I didn't feel like wearing any today. I got into my car, and I drove to the diner.

Diner

Nora

I sat in the parking lot for two minutes after I arrived. My stomach was quivering. I didn't know how Chris would react, and I still wasn't sure how I felt about the whole situation.

When I got enough courage to get out of my car and opened the door of the diner, Chris was already sitting there in the booth closest to the front door.

He had a glass of water with him. There was a pretty waitress who was leaning over the table, giving him a straight look down her cleavage. I could tell from the upper curves of her breasts that they were fake. She had platinum blonde bleached hair spiraling in curls down her back and orange skin. She had a body like a Victoria's Secret model, and I wondered what she was doing here.

I mentally slapped myself. Los Angeles had tons of beautiful people who worked in the service industry, because it had a flexible schedule that could accommodate random audition schedules. Of course this was one of the millions of would-be celebrities who put in time before they got their big break or went home to Nebrahoma Terkansas.

Chris was leaning back from her.

"Chris!" I called. He stood up as I approached, and he put a proprietary hand on my waist as he kissed my temple.

I watched the waitress's smile fade.

"Can I get you anything?" she asked. Her tone was like a three-year-old's when I told her that she couldn't have another cookie.

"Just water, please." I'd be checking it for spit.

She left without another word. Chris tugged me into his side of the booth.

He nuzzled my ear as he told me, "I missed you." My shoulders went shooting back as I felt his hand find its way between my thighs.

I pinched his wrist, but he didn't move an inch.

"Chris!" I hissed in a much different tone than I'd used earlier. Much softer.

"You can't do that here."

"I can do anything I like, baby." He gave me a slow smile, a smile that said that he would do whatever he wanted in this crowded restaurant.

"We're in public."

"That's not going to stop me." He stroked my clit with one hand.

I had to stop myself from moaning here, right now, in public.

"Chris, behave yourself...or I'll leave this restaurant right now."

The hand he still had on my waist tightened. "You're not going anywhere." There was a soft hint of steel in his voice, scarier and more intimidating than if he had shouted it.

For the first time, I wondered if Chris was dangerous.

The waitress came back with a glass of water, spilling a little on the table and splashing me.

"Oops," she said without an ounce of remorse. "My bad." She mopped it up with a rag that she had ready on her apron.

"Can I just have a burger and some fries?"

"How do you want it done?"

"Medium well."

Chris nodded. "I'll take the same."

The waitress's lips were pressed tightly together. "I'll put in your orders." She spun on her heel before she left.

"Who pissed in her Cheerios?"

I covered my face with my hand. Chris was so...loud, larger than life, embarrassing...at the same time, though, I admired how he cut through bullshit.

I turned to smile at him, and I couldn't stop myself from squeaking as he stroked my clit through my clothes.

"I can barely wait to get you into a bed," he whispered in my ear. "I've been waiting for this forever."

Our food came out in record time, and she came back with our plates. The lettuce looked a little wilted, and I wouldn't be surprised if there was spit all over mine. It tasted fine, though, and I ate it fast. I finished before Chris, who had been impeded by keeping one hand on my waist, as if I'd run if he let go.

"You like your food," he said, grinning at me.

"You calling me fat?"

"Naw. I like girls with curves." His eyes were glued to the tiny hint of cleavage peeking out. "The real kind, the kind I can squeeze." He stopped eating to adjust himself. "I like it a lot."

Chris finished his burger fast before throwing $40 on the table.

We were at his home in record time.

Reconciling

Chris

"It took so long for you to get in touch." I hungrily looked at her curves like a Catholic looked at steak on Ash Wednesday. "I need you."

I captured her mouth with mine and pressed her soft, curvy body against my body. If I had my way, I'd never let her go again.

I didn't have time to wait for a bed. I quickly did a leg sweep, and I controlled the fall. I twisted so that I was beneath her. She landed on top of me, and I had her legs apart in a half second. My body surged upwards, seeking the warmth that I hadn't felt since our night in Vegas. The night that we'd married.

"Ah," she gasped.

I shut her up by kissing her mouth, filling it with my tongue. My hands were in her hair, and I controlled the kiss, every angle, every second of it.

I kept one hand in her hair, but the other one traveled down to her ass to press her softness where I needed it the most.

I was still clothed, so I needed to fix that state of affairs.

Nora first.

I pulled off her dress, then I unclasped her bra with a single one-handed snap. Her panties were ripped off, torn so that she could never use them again.

I rolled her beneath me so that I could get naked, too. My shirt was first, then I shoved down my boxers and pants.

I felt like a lion who had been starving for far too long. I pulled her thighs apart as far as they would go.

"You ready?" I knew that she was. It was in the look in her eyes, the gleam that said that she wanted to be eaten, consumed by me. It was in the smile on her lips, a smile as old as Eve. It was the way that her pussy was dripping onto the carpet, not that I cared.

"What do you think?"

In response, I plunged inside of her.

She screamed loud enough to make the light fixtures shake a little, rattling a bit. I brought my mouth down on hers, and now she was the one filling my mouth with her tongue, taking my body as I took hers, an endless circle of pleasure.

Her hands were on my back, and I was sweating on top of her. I thrust inside again and again, but I couldn't be deep enough. I couldn't ever be deep enough. I wanted to be encoded in her DNA. I wanted her to be mine forever.

I bit her ear, then I trailed kisses down her neck to her perfect breasts. I bit them, and she hissed beneath me, sinuously twisting and milking my cock. My eyes shut as I felt a little precome shoot inside of her.

"You like this?" I pumped inside of her again, making her moan loudly. "You want it?"

"Please!"

"Please, what?" I pumped inside of her again, this time flicking her clit with my thumb.

"Make me come. Come inside of me. Now!"

"A lady's wish is my command." I rode her like I was a jockey one foot away from the finish line. I slammed into her again and again, so hard that she'd probably have bruises tomorrow. So would I.

I relentlessly played with her clit and watched her shudder and buck beneath me as I found my own

completion and spilled inside of her

delicious body.

Negotiation

Nora

"Don't. Leave. Again." Chris punctuated each word with a hard kiss, forcing my lips apart with his tongue. His hands were pinning my wrists to the bed.

"If I had my way, I'd just chain you to the bed. But I've heard that it's frowned upon these days. I can't imagine why."

I ached between my legs in the sweetest way. When I experimentally flexed my lower muscles, I realized that Chris was still inside of me. I could feel the butterfly sensation of him getting harder and harder inside of me as he recovered from his earlier orgasm.

"We have to talk," I whispered. "There are things that you need to know."

He pumped his body inside of me, and my breath caught. "I know what I need to know. And you're not abandoning me again."

My eyes closed as exquisite sensations took over my entire body. My back arched as I felt him twitch inside of my body.

He bit my neck savagely, hard enough to leave a hickey.

"That's going to leave a mark."

"Good. I want everyone to know that you're mine."

He pulled my legs up so that my knees were near my face.

He braced his body by putting his shoulders on my knees.

He withdrew slowly, and then he slammed into me, making the headboard knock against the wall. His hand found its way between my thighs to flick my clit hard. He wasn't gently rubbing it this time. He touched me in a sensitive area enough to hurt a little; there was a sweet sensation of both pain and pleasure emanating from my clit.

"You left me," Chris told me softly. "You left."

"I did, and I'm sorry." I closed my eyes as he moved inside of me. "I won't leave."

"You better not."

And if he spoke after that, I couldn't hear him. My eyes were closed, and everything else shut down. I couldn't hear, taste, or smell. All I could do was feel Chris moving inside of me intimately, connecting our bodies again and again, a puzzle piece that finally made me whole. I would enjoy it for as long as it lasted.

Tomorrow would bring its own challenges.

His mouth came down on mine brutally, just a little too hard. I could feel both passion and anger roiling inside of him, and I answered his fire with my own. We battled, Chris and I, as he took my body again and again.

I lost track of time. It seemed like he was above me for an endless eternity, stealing my breath with his kiss, blowing my mind as he entered me again and again.

My legs tensed as my body got ready to orgasm. He must have known that I was close, because he bit my shoulder hard enough to trigger me. I cried out as I felt his burning seed spill inside of my body, filling me with his essence.

The pleasure was so intense that I blacked out.

More

Chris

Her eyes were still closed as I withdrew from her soft warm body. I dove for the drawer of my nightstand.

When she heard the soft click of the handcuffs, she noticed that she was cuffed to the bed.

"Hey!" she protested indignantly. "What are you doing?"

"Handcuffing you to my bed so that you can't run away again. I told you that you wouldn't leave me again."

She shook her head. "You can't do that. People will notice that I'm gone."

"Yeah, they will. But how long would it take for them to notice?"

She smiled. "So you want to keep me in bed even though you got already got me pregnant?"

"You'd be happy," I told her, pressing my growing erection between her thighs. Then her words hit me again. "Pregnant? You're pregnant?" I looked at her body. There was a slight swell at her tummy. I felt it, and I could feel that it was solid. For some reason, thinking of my wife carrying my child had me ready yet again. I'd process all this later, but right now, I had more urgent concerns.

Nora noticed. "We just went. Are you honestly ready to go again?"

Instead of answering, I bent to suck one of her nipples into my mouth. She cried out a little. She was still covered in her juices and mine from the first round. I put my thumb on her clit and rubbed. She was screaming beneath me, tension in every muscle of her body, as I bit and licked her breasts while ruthlessly stimulating her through several orgasms.

"Too many orgasms," she told me, panting, after the fourth one. Maybe the fifth. "My mind can't take it. I've got nothing left."

I smiled and bit her ear before whispering. "You do."

With that, I parted her thick thighs and rammed all the way inside of her. We both screamed at the sensation, and her hips bucked wildly beneath me, and I breathed hard as I tried to get control of myself.

I bit her shoulder to make her slow down a little, but it just made her speed up. She pushed her hips up at me, and all I could do was drive inside of her delectable body again and again. I felt like the top of my head was going to blow off. What a way to go.

I swiveled my hips so that my cock hit Nora's G-spot. With a groan, I felt her flutter and shake around my cock, so I spilled inside of her.

When I could think again, I rolled on my side and felt for my keys.

"Kiss me." I suspended my body above her, just a hair away from her mouth. She tilted her chin up, and we had a soft, tender kiss. It was funny, because we were married and having a kid together, but Nora hadn't initiated a lot of kisses.

I bit her neck again in the same spot as before, and then I unlocked her handcuffs.

The whole room smelled like sex. I wanted the whole house to smell like it. I made a mental note to have her on every surface in my home.

Right now, though, we were sweaty and sticky. I brought her into my bathroom.

"You have a Jacuzzi?"

"Yup."

I put her inside, and then I turned on the water and the jets.

I climbed in and pulled Nora into my lap so that she was straddling me.

"I don't think that we'll get very clean if you want to keep me in this position."

My hips bucked up towards her. "I don't think we'll get that clean."

One hand parted her lower lips while the other grabbed the hair at the back of her head. I pulled her down on my waiting erection.

She wiggled a little bit on top of me, and I started panting. She began swirling her hips, and I couldn't think of anything but the exquisite

sensation of Nora moving on top of

me.

   She bit my ear and shoulder, and

I was done. With a shout, I spilled

into her again. My eyes were closed

as she held onto my shoulders and

rode me. My dick was sensitive that it

was painful, but I wouldn't give up a

moment of the time that I got to

spend inside of Nora. She grunted her

way through her own orgasm. When

she was done, she put her head on

my shoulder. I put my arms around her, stroking her back.

"I'm exhausted," she whispered. "You wore me out."

I was pretty tired, too, but I couldn't stop a grin of pure male pride from curving my lips upwards.

With Nora still in my lap, I turned off the water and jets and opened up the drain.

She clung to me as I stood up. I snagged a towel from the rack, then I threw her into my bed, still wet from the Jacuzzi.

"There's water everywhere," she protested softly, yawning. I bundled her up in the towel. I kissed her temple.

"Sleep."

I walked back into the bathroom to dry myself off.

I caught a glimpse of myself in the partially foggy mirror. I had a bite mark on my shoulder, and I wished that I could keep it forever. I knew that Nora enjoyed sex with me, but I was determined to show her that we had more than that.

Pancakes

Nora

When I woke up, the first thing I noticed was how sore I was between my thighs.

The second thing I noticed was the smell of bacon.

For the first morning in a long time, I didn't feel like I needed to throw up immediately.

I went into Chris' closet and pulled out a soft, huge t-shirt that smelled like him before heading towards the kitchen.

When I got there, Chris was turning off the stove and sliding pancakes onto a plate along with a little bacon. He was totally naked, so I admired the perfect curve of his ass for a moment.

"Good morning," I told him.

He set the plates down and went towards me.

"You're up. Move in with me. I want you to be here every morning." Before I had a chance to say a word, he picked me up and kissed me, pushing his tongue between my lips. I didn't even worry about morning mouth because Chris tasted divine.

The kiss went on and on until I felt my butt come down on his granite countertop.

I squealed from how cold it was, but he didn't stop kissing me. He parted my thighs and pushed a finger inside of me. His thumb circled my clit while he stimulated my G-spot. I felt myself get soaking wet, and I pulsed around his finger.

He withdrew it, and then I felt the head of his cock probing my entrance. I tried to scoot towards it, but he shoved me back as he thrust inside of my body.

He bit my neck hard enough to hurt, ad I dimly remembered that he had bitten it in the same spot before. That mark was going to be huge.

Speaking of huge, his cock was pulling me apart. No matter how many times I had him, my body still burned when he entered me.

His thumb pushed against my clit again, and I gasped as I felt myself fall off of the cliff, spiraling downwards.

His tongue thrust deeply into my mouth as he spilled into my body.

He pulled back, and I opened my eyes.

"Wow."

"Breakfast?"

I blinked, but he was already putting our plates on the table. Both of them were enough for three lumberjacks.

"I can't eat that much," I told him, feeling his warm come oozing between my legs. "And I'll get come on your chair."

He raised one eyebrow at me. With a swift move, he pulled me into his lap.

"There. Now you don't have to worry about getting come on my chair." He licked my neck. "Now eat."

I leaned forward and closed my eyes as I tasted the fluffy pancake.

The maple syrup wasn't the store-bought weak kind. It was the real kind that you'd buy from a farmer's market.

"Oh my, Chris. I didn't know that you could cook."

"I can only cook breakfast. Besides scrambled eggs, this is about it."

"I like it." I smiled and ate some more. I rubbed the inside of his thigh, and I felt his dick stiffen a little against my ass.

As we continued eating, his cock got harder and harder. I would not deny that I was rubbing a little bit, shifting my weight in his lap. It was a fun game.

When I had finished the last bite of my bottom pancake, he immediately stole the plate from me and pushed his plate to the side.

"Tease. You're going to pay for that."

My cheek rested against the cool, smooth wood as he lifted his t-shirt to expose my ass. He spanked one cheek, and then he spanked the other. He parted my thighs easily. His huge hand came to wrap around my neck, and his thumb and middle finger pushed against my clavicle as he slid my body back towards his dick.

I had zero control in this position, facedown on the table. He pounded my body in a fast, hard rhythm. I supposed that I had made him wait.

I felt my body turn into a puddle of happiness. I closed my eyes and just felt Chris entering me over and over again, moving my body as he liked. My clit was rubbing against the edge of the table.

He leaned down to bite my shoulder, and I squeaked and clenched my muscles around him.

That was enough for him to pick up the pace and ram into me harder than before. I couldn't hold on any longer and felt my body climax. I gasped for air as I felt him release inside of me, filling me with his hot seed.

He left my body, and I just lay there on the table. If I was going to keep doing this, I'd need to train. He was wearing me out.

I heard water running, and then I felt a warm, wet towel between my thighs. It felt soothing and nice, making my back muscles relax slowly.

I heard the soft landing of the towel when he threw it away.

I put my hands on either side of my face, preparing to stand, when I felt Chris' tongue slide inside of me.

"Chris!"

He didn't say a word, just pulled my thighs a little further apart. He ate me out while he pushed me rhythmically against the edge of the table so that my clit was called into action again.

One hand went to the base of my spine to rub my sacrum. I felt pure, golden joy release inside of my body, filling me from top to bottom. I felt like I should be glowing.

My legs started shaking, and then my whole body shook as I

climaxed again. I'd had more climaxes in the last 24 hours than I did in a normal year.

"You're a better breakfast than anything that I could cook."

Chris' arms pulled me up by my shoulders, and my feet touched the ground. He squeezed one of my breasts as he asked, "What are you going to do today?"

My phone buzzed. He tried to steal it, but I went and checked it.

"It's Laila."

He let go of me.

"What does she want?"

"She wants to meet for brunch. You down?"

"Yeah."

I texted her that I'd show up. Chris' phone buzzed.

"Trouble." Chris' eyebrow went up. "He wants me to come to brunch."

"How surprised do you think they'll be if we show up together?"

"Only way to figure that out is to do it." He squeezed one of my breasts while staring into my eyes, making warmth pool inside of my body.

He pushed me back on the counter. My nervousness about meeting Laila and Trouble for the first time as a couple melted away as he made me melt into a puddle full of glowing light.

We were late getting into the car to meet Laila at our favorite bagel place.

Laila's Pregnancy

Chris

Laila and Trouble were holding hands, sitting side by side at the table at the bagel shop. I looked at their interlocked hands and grimaced.

"Barf."

"Get used to it, buddy. We're married, and we have other news."

"Yeah?"

"I'm having a baby!"

I was very glad that I was sitting down, because I felt like a puppet with my strings cut.

"What? How did that happen?" I blinked rapidly, and I looked between them.

"High school health class taught you how that happened, dog. But yeah, we're going to expand our family. Congratulate us, bro."

"Yeah, congratulations, whatever." I felt slightly dizzy as if Trouble had punched me in the face.

In a way, I felt like he had. I was still adjusting to my baby sister being married, and wham!

Kiddo on board.

I cleared my throat and looked at Nora. If there was a right moment, it was right here. Right now.

"You want to?"

Laila looked between us, and the skin next to her eyes tightened.

"What's going on? What's wrong?"

Nora smiled a Pan Am smile, the kind of smile that only moved her lips. "I'm expecting, too."

Laila glared at me. "Did you...?"

"Yes."

She leaned back. "Oh wow. But you two are really different, because Trouble and I are married, and you two are just seeing...each..."

She looked at both of us staring at the table.

"Oh my gosh. Nora. Your hand."

Nora looked at her wedding ring as if she had zero clue how it got there.

"You're married?" Laila shook her head like a dog shaking off water. "You two are married? When? How? What?"

Trouble squeezed her hand. "I didn't know that you got hitched."

"It wasn't...planned." Nora's voice was so quiet that I could barely hear her. "It just happened."

"And now you're having a baby."

"Yes."

"What are you guys planning?"

"We're taking each day as it comes."

I was silent. Nora knew how I felt about all of this. She was my wife, and she was carrying my child. I would prefer for her to move in with me, but she probably wanted to stay in school for the time being. I just considered myself lucky that she hadn't aborted our baby before I even knew about it. We'd had a discussion over breakfast...a one-sided discussion, since I'd distracted her with sex, but I knew that she was probably moving in.

"Where are you guys even going to live? Nora's still in school. Are you moving in with her?"

I snorted. "No. She lives in a tiny studio. No way."

"I'm not living with him." Nora pointed at me. "He's a night owl."

We hadn't really talked about it. "I am not. It's not my fault that you get up at ass o'clock every day." Laila had told me a long time ago that Nora liked to do pre-dawn yoga.

"Not mine that you go to bed around that time, either."

We looked away from each other.

Trouble cleared his throat. "Okay, then. Laila and I need to go to an appointment with a midwife to discuss our options."

I felt like he had punched me in the gut. I guessed that I needed to get involved with a lot of the prenatal care, and he was obviously a good dad already.

I had no idea about any of this. I wasn't one of those guys who cooed over tiny babies. Every time that I held one, people yelled at me about supporting the head and neck. I didn't know anything about babies, except that they weighed about the same as a fish that was keeper-sized.

"See you guys," Nora said, smiling and waving. I wished that she smiled at me, but she hadn't really been all that friendly after we'd gotten married. It was true that marriage ruined everything.

Laila and Trouble left. I opened my wallet to throw a few bills on the table, not bothering to wait for the check.

"Let's head out. I guess we need to talk."

Fatherhood

Chris

Nora and I walked out of the restaurant, and I couldn't hold myself back anymore.

"How the fuck do you handle a baby? I know shit about having a child."

"Language!" Nora hissed at me. "Do you want our baby coming out of the wound and saying a curse word as his first word?"

"Do you know the gender already?"

"No, I just have a feeling. Do you care either way?"

I thought about it. A little boy to climb trees. A little girl to chase around the yard, pigtails flying behind her.

"No."

"Good." She sighed. "I scheduled an appointment for this afternoon to confirm my pregnancy. You want to come with?"

"Yeah." I had a few meetings scheduled this afternoon, so I pulled out my phone and texted my assistant to cancel them because I was unavoidably detained. I slipped the phone back into my pocket.

Nora was frowning at me. "What?" I'd just cleared my schedule for her, and she was acting like I'd done something wrong.

"I don't want you to use your phone when you should be paying attention to the baby. What kind of father would you be if you never paid attention to your baby? Are you going to be another Elon Musk, emailing on his phone while he spends time with his kids? Always needing a nanny to keep an eye on them?"

I shrugged. "I don't know yet. I haven't spent any time with little kids, especially not babies. I think of them as poop and barf machines."

"You might want to change your mindset, because you're about to get your own poop and barf machine."

I eyed her stomach with its gentle curve. "I guess so." I reached out a hand to touch the lump, and she took a half step back.

"Did you drive here?"

"Yeah, I'm parked down the block. I can meet you at the doctor's office. I'll give you the address." She whipped out her phone.

I heard my phone buzz when I received her text.

"See you soon."

She headed in the opposite direction from where my car was parked.

I walked up several flights of stairs to find my car.

The baby was becoming more and more real to me. He or she was going to be a tiny human being who would be my responsibility.

I was terrified of being a father more than I'd been afraid of anything in my entire life. I'd lived my life prepping for swimming competitions, so I was no stranger to a healthy dose of fear and a little performance anxiety. But this was another level. A tiny human being would depend on me and his mother for his existence.

Man, was I lost.

I got into my car, set up my GPS, and saw that the doctor's office was about 5 minutes away.

I turned on the radio but didn't really hear the music.

When I got there, Nora was already waiting outside.

"Hey. Let's go."

I followed her inside, and I sat in a chair while she got checked in.

First Sonogram

Nora

I gave Lisa, the receptionist, my insurance card so that she could make a copy. She gave me a huge clipboard in return so that I could take a little survey.

A little blue pen with a daisy taped to the top was attached to the clipboard with a length of yarn.

"The nurse will be with you shortly. You can wait with your husband in the waiting room."

Husband.

I didn't know how insurance worked. I didn't even know if Chris had bothered to get insurance for his company, because I knew that he worked for himself. I had PPO insurance from my school, and it was enough to pay for a doctor's visit now. My family was nowhere near as wealthy as the Kings were, but we did okay. My father wasn't much of one, but if providing money for what I needed were the only measure of fatherhood, he'd win.

I sat down next to Chris. I checked things off, feeling very self-conscious. We were married, but he was probably learning more about me from the boxes that I checked and the family history I noted on this form that he'd ever learn from me. It's not like we talked a lot. I didn't know all that much about Chris.

"Nora? Is there a Nora?"

I stood up, knocking the clipboard to the floor in my haste to get away from Chris. My face heated up as I bent to pick up the clipboard.

"I'm Nora."

"Will your husband be coming back with us?"

My husband? Right, Chris. He was rubbing the back of his neck. The OBGYN's office was all about lady parts.

"Do you want to come back with me, Chris?"

"Yeah."

He stood up. He was so tall that he blocked the light behind him, appearing as a dark silhouette.

"Come on."

The nurse brought us to the back. She took my vitals, and she weighed me. I burned with shame, but Chris did his best impression of someone who wasn't listening.

She asked me questions about my habits, and I answered them to the best of my ability. I wished I hadn't prohibited Chris from using his phone. Going to the doctor with someone I barely knew was one of the most humiliating experiences of my entire life.

When the nurse was done, she told me, "The doctor will be in soon."

I heard them talking in the hallway. Chris put his hand on mine. "It'll be okay." He kissed the back of my hand. "I can't wait to see you on your back again." He winked at me.

My face was in flames when the doctor opened the door.

"Hello. How are you doing today, Nora?"

"I'm great, Dr. Watson." I shook his hand. "This is my husband, Chris." Chris shook Dr. Watson's hand, too.

"What brings you here today, Nora?"

"I think I'm pregnant."

"What symptoms do you have?"

"A little weight gain, and I've been barfing for the past few mornings. I used a home pregnancy test, but I want confirmation."

"Have you been trying to have a child, Mr. and Mrs. King?"

Chris choked a little. "No."

"No, we haven't been trying to have a kid."

"Oh, I see…a Disneyland baby."

"I beg your pardon?" What was that?

"A honeymoon baby, when you just get so carried away."

My face felt hot again, and Chris was blushing, too.

"I…um…we…yes."

"It's perfectly fine. In this age of family planning, plenty of people have kids that they weren't planning on having. We can do a quick test with some of your blood, or we can do a very fast sonogram to check if you have someone in there." The doctor touched my little bump.

"Let's just do a quick sonogram."

"Lift your shirt, please, and lay back on the bed." The doctor patted the big bed.

I hopped up, and the doctor made it so that I was at a 45 degree angle. She had a bunch of gel, and I gasped a little when she put it on my stomach.

"Yes, sorry, the gel is a little cold." The doctor pulled out a little attachment, and rubbed it around on my stomach. The doctor was staring at the screen, and Chris and I were look at it, too.

There was a little thing moving around on the screen.

"It looks like an alien," Chris said.

"Chris!" I cried. "Why would you say that?"

"It does."

The doctor laughed. "The baby doesn't look like too much at this stage. But your baby looks just fine. If you want, we can all hear the baby's heartbeat." The doctor turned up a dial, and we heard the baby's little hummingbird heart inside of the room.

All of us were quiet for a moment. Our baby was a real person.

"Would you like a picture to take home?"

"Yes, please." I didn't know if I could believe the evidence of my eyes and ears. I knew that I'd look at this picture over and over again. The doctor gave me the snapshot, and I saw my little peanut in my stomach. The doctor gave me a paper towel to wipe away some of the goo, and then I lowered my shirt. I felt shy in front of Chris, but it wasn't anything that he hadn't seen before.

I went out to the front and paid my copay. Then, Chris and I went out to our cars. There was a bench near the parking garage, and Chris tugged my wrist so that I sat down next to him.

"You have my baby. What do you want to do?"

"I'm not sure." I bit my lip. "I didn't know for sure, and now that we do..."

I took the little sonogram picture out of my purse. "I have a little one."

"Yup."

"Can I have some time to think about it?"

"Sure. How about we have breakfast together tomorrow? Let's sleep on it."

I nodded. "Yeah. I can meet you at the diner near my house at 8 AM tomorrow morning."

"Sounds good to me. I'll clear my schedule. You're the most important thing for me right now." His big hand squeezed my shoulder, and he turned away.

On the Run

Nora

A wave of terror washed over me. I knew that I had no plans to see him for breakfast tomorrow.

I had class, but somehow it seemed that my accidental pregnancy was more important than going to class.

I needed to get away. There was a little resort in the mountains that I had gone to when I wanted to get away from LA. I guessed that I'd head there.

I called in sick to the university, and I sent emails to my professors that I was sick and needed to get all the course materials. They sent me their Powerpoint presentations. I'd read them while I was away at the tiny resort.

It didn't take me too long to drive there. Outside of LA, the traffic cleared up a lot. So then I drove on the winding mountain roads to the tiny resort that nobody knew about but me. Even Laila didn't know about my secret place.

I got a room and passed out. Pregnancy was making me tired.

* * *

The next morning, I went down to the dining room for a little breakfast. The thought of eating bacon made my stomach turn, but I knew that I could eat some toast and maybe a little fruit.

There were only a few people in the dining room. I guessed that most people just got room service.

There was a guy wearing a suit in the corner reading a paper. There were three empty tables near him, and I snagged a chair with my fruit plate. I was drinking my glass of apple juice when I heard Chris say, "Hello."

I sprayed apple juice everywhere. The glass slipped from my hand, and it poured all over the carpet.

I watched as Chris brought the newspaper down.

"What are you doing here?"

"Did you think that you could run and hide so easily? You know that I have whatever resources I want in order to find you."

"But nobody knows where I am."

He raised one eyebrow, and I flushed. "Except for you."

"You have a cell phone. It's the best tracking device devised by man."

"I don't even have a signal half the time out here. I have to make calls over Wi-Fi if I don't want them to be dropped."

He shrugged. "I'm not really constrained by those limitations." If Chris hadn't been constrained before, why hadn't he looked for me for the first three months after we got married? But I was grateful for the space that he'd left me nonetheless; I'd needed to make a decision on my own without any pressure from him. If he was in the room, he just assumed that he could make all the decisions.

"I guess."

I used my napkin to wipe myself up. Someone on the hotel staff had an ultra-absorbent micro-fiber towel on the ground, soaking up my spilled apple juice. I felt like a huge klutz.

"I'm so sorry," I told the young waitress. She couldn't be older than 20.

"It's fine, ma'am. All done." She sprayed something on the carpet and was gone.

"What are you even doing here?"

"You said that we'd have breakfast. I guess that we're just going to do it somewhere else."

I shook my head. "You found me in a half instant. Why didn't you do this when we were first married?"

"I didn't know that you were carrying my child until yesterday," Chris told me coldly. "And now the rules have changed. Before, annulment and/or divorce were a possibility. Now they are not."

"Hey there. I'm pretty sure I get half the say in this marriage, and I think those are still on the table."

"They aren't."

I bristled. "What do you mean, 'they aren't?'"

"We're never getting divorced. We have a baby."

"You didn't really...we're not even really married! We got married by Elvis."

"But we are married." Chris leaned forward in his seat. "Jalicia might be my dad's second wife, but he stayed married to his first wife, my mother, until death separated them. I know that I take marriage really seriously."

"We were married in the Chapel of Love! That's not a real marriage."

"It is to me."

"Are you joking? You've had more girls than you can even count, and suddenly marriage is everything to you? We got drunk in Vegas and made a stupid mistake."

"We're not divorcing. We're going to stay married and raise our baby together."

"There is no us!" My voice was getting loud enough to get some glances from the other people in the dining room. I quieted down a little bit. "You're barely my husband. I have no desire to stay married to you. We'll figure something out for the baby, and I know that Laila is going to be over the moon to have a playmate for her little one. It'll be fine."

"We're staying married," Chris parroted. "That's the end of it."

I crossed my arms and lost my appetite. "Marriage takes two people, buddy, and don't forget it."

Chris folded his newspaper neatly, and he laid it to the side. "Are you done with your breakfast?"

The fruit that had looked so fresh and nice only minutes ago looked repulsive now. "Yes."

Chris laid a $100 bill on the table. "I'm sure that this will take care of it." He signaled for a waiter and handed the money to him.

"Let's go."

I wasn't sure what had me trailing him out of the restaurant. I didn't bring much to the resort. They had a store where I could buy a change of clothes, and I hadn't bothered to go home yesterday. I just ran straight to the mountains, so I didn't really have anything of my own in my hotel room.

I got outside, and I realized that my car was gone.

"What the heck did you do to my car? Where is it?"

"I had it towed this morning." Chris' tone sounded like it was to be expected. Like I was a fool to expect my car to be where I left it yesterday.

"Listen up."

"Get into my car."

"No!" I shouted. "I'm going back in there, and I'm going back to my room. I don't want to talk to you right now. You're the one who got me into this mess, and I don't want to deal with you."

"If you don't want to do this the nice way…" Chris came by me and stuffed me in the back seat, then shut the door. I tried to open the door, but it had the child locks on. I tried to get over the center console, but Chris stopped me.

"Buckle up. Don't want to hurt the baby."

I crossed my arms. "No."

"Don't be a child." His voice was cold, stone cold. It wasn't even like this when I'd met him again.

He turned on the car, and we pulled out. When we went around the first mountain road curve, my shoulder hit the window. Hard. I winced. That would leave a mark. I buckled up.

Chris turned on the radio, and we were quiet as we made our way back to LA.

I fell asleep in the backseat.

Staying Married

Nora

When I woke up, I wasn't in the mountains anymore. I was at Chris' solo place, a nice mansion in Bel Air.

There was a bottle of water next to my bed. I drank a swig, then I got out of bed.

I felt so tired, as if I wanted to go back and sleep in the fluffy bed again.

I could hear Chris crashing around in the kitchen. Something smelled good. Pork, maybe? For the first time in a while, meat smelled good to me.

I walked down the stairs and headed towards Chris' kitchen.

"How do you feel about pork braciole?"

"Braciole? I've never had that before."

"It's just pork pounded thin and rolled around chard, provolone, Parmesan, bread crumbs, prosciutto, and a little egg to make it all stick together."

"Sounds great to me." Suddenly I was ravenous. My stomach growled. "When will it be ready?"

"Maybe another minute. Could you get out two plates?"

I looked around, and all of his cabinets had glass fronts. There was a pile of plates, and I had to stand on my tiptoes in order to reach the dishes.

I got two of them out, and I brought them to Chris. He pulled the braciole out of the pan and slid it onto our plates. He had some kind of tomato sauce in a little sauce pot, and he ladled it onto our plates.

"Smells heavenly. I didn't even know that you could cook." The spices in that tomato sauce were insanely great.

Chris shrugged. "My mom made me learn. After my freshman swim season, she got tired of feeding what she called bottomless pits. You know I had a lot of the team over all the time."

"Yeah, totally."

"I got pretty proficient at cooking stuff in our slow-cooker so that we could just heat it up on the stove and eat."

"Cool."

"Yeah, and in college, there were a lot of nights when I'd get drunk-hungry around 3 AM, when only McDonald's was open. I'm a swimmer, so..."

"McD's wasn't your best friend."

"Not if I wanted to win, no." Chris shrugged. "I can cook."

Chris' ability to cook was sexier than any tattoos or any motorcycles, though he had tats and a bike.

We sat down in his breakfast nook, and he had already set the table with forks and knives.

I cut off a little of the braciole, and it was fantastic.

"Oh my god, I've never eaten this before, but I want to eat it every day."

Chris grinned at me. "I'm glad that you like it."

We ate in silence for a little while before Chris stopped to take a sip of his milk.

"We've got to talk."

My shoulders instantly tensed up. I knew that we had to talk, but I'd run away yesterday to get away from this conversation. I tucked a strand of hair behind my ear and nodded. "We do."

He leaned forward. "I know that I might have sounded a little bit like a caveman at the resort, but I really believe that we can make this thing work. I would take great care of our kid, you know that."

I nodded. "I do."

"So you can move in...we can figure it out as we go, like we told Laila."

I dropped my fork and covered my eyes with my hand. "Let me think." When he was staring at me with his laser-focused blue eyes, it was hard for me to figure out what I wanted to do. What I really wanted was to do a replay of our honeymoon, as brief as it had been.

"You can set the terms," he told me. "Tell me what you need, and I'll make it happen."

"I want some autonomy."

"Noted. What else?"

"I'd like to not worry about providing for the baby."

Chris snorted. "What kind of man do you think I am? Of course I'll provide for the baby. That was never in question. What else?"

All the tension seeped out of my body. I really thought that we could make this work.

I smiled at him, and I wasn't shocked when he came around the table and brought his mouth down on mine.

He pulled me out of the seat and carried me to his bedroom.

Tied Up

Chris

I put her facedown on my bed.

"Do you trust me?"

"Yes," she whispered.

"Then keep your hands where they are." I got soft cloth ties out of my nightstand, and I tied her hands together after I pulled them above her head.

I quickly and methodically pulled all of her clothes off. I could not get them all of the way off, but she was naked enough for my purposes.

I took in the feast in front of me. She was so beautiful, and she held herself like she didn't know how fucking stunning she was. She was everything that I needed and never knew I did.

I petted her pussy, and I was gratified to hear her sharp intake of breath. I stroked her clit as I decided to explore her pussy lips with my mouth.

She moaned as I pushed my tongue inside of her, aiming straight for her G-spot. From the volume of her moans, I knew that I'd hit the target.

She shook her way through one orgasm, then another. And another.

"No more," she begged. "Too much."

"Baby, I'm not done."

She didn't have time to protest as I rolled her on her back and pushed two fingers inside of her waiting body. Her hips came off the bed, and I pushed her pelvis back down with the two fingers which were inside of her. She screamed as she found the strength inside to go over the cliff another time. I stroked inside of her as her sensitive body pushed her towards another peak.

"You want me to stop? You don't want more."

"You bastard...don't you dare not finish."

"What's that?"

She arched basically her entire body off of the bed like a bow, trying to catch me. I took a few steps back.

"Get back here right now." Her bound hands were suddenly around my neck, and she jumped so that her legs were around my hips.

I pushed and slid inside of her, and then I kissed my wife. She moaned into my mouth, and I fucked her with my tongue.

We crashed into the bed, the two of us, and I heard the bed frame snap from the force. I was willing to break a dozen beds to get inside of her just once.

I held her wrists down above her head as I worshipped her perfect, full breasts. She shivered beneath me, and I bit her right nipple fiercely. I looked down at my handiwork, and I loved the mark of my mouth on my wife.

I pushed my hips against her, and she groaned as her back arched. I tucked my face between her neck and shoulder, and I gave her everything that I had. Every inch of me, every bit of me that I could pour into her, more than I could give and live — everything went into my wife. She was my present and future. I'd had plenty of women in the past, but Nora would be my last.

When I was done releasing inside of her, and once she was done clenching her tight body on mine, I rolled over and untied her hands.

"What do you want to do today?"

Facebook Official

Nora

"Well, first, I'm going to take a shower."

I saw Chris' eyes light up and shook my head. "No. If we shower together, we're not going to get anything done today."

He smiled ruefully. "True."

"You can go to work. I'll go shopping for some maternity clothes and maybe start looking at stuff for the baby."

"What do you need clothes for? What you're wearing now looks fine to me. Naked would be better." He reached for me, and I slapped his hands away.

"You can't keep me naked all the time, and I'm eventually going to get a baby bump that's too big to even fit inside of your t-shirts. I've got to get clothes."

He shrugged. "Okay." He reached for his wallet, and he took out a black credit card. It was an AmEx.

"Is that a—?"

"Centurion Card? Yeah. It's yours. See?" He handed it to me, and I read my name. Mrs. Nora King.

"Buy whatever you need. Hell, buy half a dozen things that the baby doesn't need. Go wild."

I blinked. "Carte blanche isn't a good idea when a pregnant woman is nesting."

He shrugged. "I can afford it."

He could, and I knew it, too. I'd buy the necessities now, but I also knew that I didn't have a good idea of what the necessities were. I wouldn't be surprised if I had to have some of the stuff delivered to the house because it wouldn't fit into my car.

The card made something else real to me: Chris and I were going to stay married. And if that was the case...

"Can we make our marriage Facebook official?"

Chris blinked. "What?"

"Well, it's not like we invited anybody we knew to our wedding. And I didn't know if we were going to go the distance. But now that we're definitely staying married..."

"Yeah." Chris picked up his phone and pulled up the Facebook app. "Relationship status: married to Nora." He tapped the screen a few times before he said, "Done."

I felt like a huge weight had lifted off of my shoulders. Now that the question of my marriage was settled, I could focus on this path, on this future.

I went into the guest bedroom and soaked in the tub while I thought about what it would mean to be married to Chris for the foreseeable future...at least the next 18 years. I put a hand on my stomach. There was a tiny human growing inside of me. I knew that Chris would be a fun dad, and I just hoped that I'd be a good mother.

My fingers were pruny by the time I got out of the tub. When I peeked into the garage, Chris' car was gone. He must have showered and left.

I didn't have any of my own clothes besides what I'd worn yesterday. I raided Chris' closet again, taking his smallest t-shirt. I put on a pair of his basketball shorts, which were the length of Capris on me. I shook my head. Chris was so tall. The jock strap felt weird, but I had to make the best of the situation. My first stop was definitely to buy some more clothes. I needed to go home to pick up all my stuff and pack it up. I understood from the way that Chris was talking about me putting together a nursery that he assumed that I was moving in. Living together would probably be the best for everyone involved.

I pulled my hair into a quick bun. I didn't put on any makeup. I looked like a complete hot mess, dressed in a baggy shirt and shorts that were too long on me, but it'd have to do. Surely the people at Target wouldn't

faint from the sight of my hideous
clothing.

Target

Nora

I went into Target and signed into KickShop, which was connected to my Facebook account. I got points for running around Target and finding items while I was there.

I headed straight for the maternity section. There were really cute Liz Lange tops. I'd never fit into them before, but I would now.

I picked up a few tops so that I could try them on in the dressing room.

The dressing room attendant barely looked at me when I asked for a number. She handed it to me, and she texted somebody on her phone. Like nearly every retail dressing room attendant, she was checked out.

I went into the dressing room. Only one stall was taken, so I went into a roomy stall, closed the curtain, and got naked.

Abruptly, the curtain was pushed aside. I covered myself.

"Hey!"

I had a single second to notice that a tall blonde girl was in front of me before I blacked out from a punch.

* * *

When I woke up, everything was dark. I blinked a few times, and I realized that something was over my head. I struggled, and I felt that my hands were bound together.

"Oh, you're awake."

I stilled. "Where am I?"

"Somewhere that Chris won't find you."

"Who are you?"

"Jordana."

Something sparked in the back of my mind. "Chris' ex-girlfriend from high school? The one that got pregnant?" The bunny boiler who terrified Laila with her insanity? I kept that last one to myself.

"That's me." She laughed bitterly. "Why can you remember better than Chris can?"

"What are you talking about?"

"I'm talking about waking up with Chris King in my bed again, only for him to have no idea who I am." I could feel her rage pouring out of her, almost physically burning me.

"We can work something out."

"You're married to him."

"Yeah, but it's only because of the baby."

"Baby? You're having his baby?" I heard the interest in her voice, and I winced underneath the hood. I probably should've kept that under wraps.

"Yeah."

She touched my tummy, and I cringed away from her cold hand. "I just thought that you were fat."

"Hey!"

"Don't make me knock you out again," she said with no emotion at all, as if she were an android. It made my whole body feel cold. I said a quick prayer to anybody who could hear me.

"You're married because you have a baby?"

It was more complicated than that, but I just said, "Yes."

She left me alone, finally. I breathed a few deep breaths, trying to calm down. I heard her get close to me again, and I screamed as I heard a knife being unsheathed.

"I want to see your face." The hood came off of my face. Jordana's eyes were beyond crazy — she looked extremely calm, which just served to terrify me.

"What are you going to do?"

"Get rid of your marriage." She smiled. "And your baby."

I screamed as the knife came down on my unprotected stomach.

Blood

Nora

I stared at the blade cutting into me. I felt physical pain of course. Jordana had sliced through my intestines, but that didn't really concern me. I recognized that it should, but all of my concern was elsewhere.

"My baby," I gasped.

"Die, bitch," Jordana spat as she sliced me a second time while pulling the knife out for a second blow.

I closed my eyes and made my peace as I waited for the second blow to come. I wished that I hadn't run away from Chris, because our baby and marriage had been stolen before we'd really had the time to get used to it.

The second blow never came.

I heard the door burst open, and I opened my eyes. There was a man wearing a black vest that said SWAT across his chest.

About 30 seconds ago, that would've meant everything to me. But now that my baby was dead, I was a casually disinterested observer.

I watched as they tackled Jordana with her knife safely knocked out of her hand, cuffing her as they read her Miranda rights.

I was quiet as Chris came running into the room, kneeling by my side.

"You're bleeding," he said. "Oh my god, you're bleeding so much. We need an ambulance." He took out a pocket knife and cut the zip ties that held my hands over my head.

I was quiet and still, watching him from what seemed to be a long way away. This man, my husband, meant a lot to me just a few minutes ago, but I couldn't make myself move or care.

"Nora? Are you okay?" He laughed a laugh without any mirth in it. "Besides this massive wound?"

I blinked at him.

"Nora?" He frowned. "Baby, are you okay?"

I just stared right back at him. I knew that I should be talking, reassuring him that I was just fine, but the truth was that I wasn't fine at all. My baby was dead inside of me. My little one was gone. I didn't need a doctor or nurse to tell me what I knew in my heart.

Dead.

"Nora, you're scaring me. Tell me that you're okay. We'll get an ambulance here right away. You'll be fine."

I closed my eyes and drifted away. Far away.

Hospital

Chris

I paced around the hallway, unable to sit in a chair in the hospital and watch Nora sleep anymore. The nurse had kicked me out of the room so that she and the doctor could take care of Nora and check on her.

The doctor came out of her room.

"Oh, Mr. King."

I zoomed towards Nora's OBGYN. "What's going on? Is the baby okay?"

She shook her head. "I regret to inform you that your child is dead."

I felt like someone sucker punched me in the gut.

"The baby is dead?"

"Yes." She touched my shoulder. "I know it's hard. Loss of a child is never easy."

"Can I go in?"

She nodded. "Nora's physically fine. She's healing nicely, and I think that we'll be able to discharge her in another day. But emotionally, losing a child is a wound that takes a lot longer to heal than a knife wound."

I swallowed past the lump in my throat.

"Understood."

I walked into Nora's room, and I knew that she was awake.

She was staring at the ceiling, still not talking. She hadn't spoken since we found her.

"Hey, Nora." I took her hand. She didn't pull away or squeeze it. She just kept staring straight up, as if I never came into the room at all.

* * *

A day passed, and Nora was still unresponsive. Physically, she was good enough that the doctor discharged her. I took her home, and she still said nothing. I got more and more worried as time went on.

She didn't want to eat much, and it was all I could do to get her to eat one meal a day.

She spent all of her time curled up in a ball in bed. Her skin was ashy, and she was lifeless in a way that made me worry.

I tried to get Laila to come in, but Nora had showed her only sign of life when she insisted that she didn't want to see Laila. She pointed out how tactless I was to make her see someone who was happily pregnant.

I hadn't tried to get Laila to visit since then.

* * *

It had been two weeks since she lost the baby. I went to her bedroom, but she was already in the bathroom.

I waited for to get out, and I was surprised to see that she had dressed herself for the first time since she lost the baby. She looked like she was ready for the day, ready to face everything.

"You good?"

Breakthrough

Chris

I saw a tear make its way down Nora's cheek.

"Nora. Talk to me."

"I feel like I failed my baby in the most fundamental way possible." The whisper was so quiet that I could barely hear it, and the quiet sob that came after broke my heart.

I took her into my arms and kissed her cheek. "It's not your fault."

"It is." She sobbed in earnest now, burying her face in my shoulder. While I wasn't happy that she was crying, I was glad that she was finally talking.

Her body was shaking with the force of her sobs.

"A mother's first duty is to protect her baby, and I couldn't." She was a little muffled, but I could still hear her.

"You weren't to blame. All of this is Jordana's fault. She's going to jail for life since she killed the baby."

"I couldn't save the baby. My baby is dead." I felt grief come over me like a wave. I knew that she was drowning, and I stood up with her in my arms.

"I know where we need to go."

"Go? Where?"

"You'll see." I looked at what Nora was wearing. She was wearing a thin nightgown that looked like a very casual dress. "We're going to the mall."

"The mall? Why? So we can return all the baby stuff?" Nora's arms wrapped around herself. "I don't want to."

"No, we're not returning stuff. We're taking my bike."

Nora smiled. It was a small smile, one that barely picked up the edges of her mouth, but I saw just a glimpse of Nora's normal self.

"I'll enjoy that."

I went to the bike helmets that I stashed near the door and tossed one to her.

"Let's go."

I was out the door, and I heard Nora come behind me. She locked the door, and I knew that we were going to be okay.

She got on the back of my bike, and her arms wrapped around my middle. Our grief had been difficult to work through, but I knew that with Nora by my side, I could face anything. Without her, it was a toss-up.

My bike roared to life, and I got on the road. There was nothing like the feeling of the world flying by you. You can't replicate the feeling of being on a motorcycle by opening your car window or riding in a convertible.

I felt alive and free, and I hoped that Nora felt a little bit of that, too.

We got to the mall, and I parked in motorcycle parking.

I kept my arm around her small shoulders as we walked around inside. Walking around the mall wasn't much, but it let me know that Nora was taking her first steps towards recovery.

All she wanted to do was walk around and look at stuff. I'd hated going to the mall with my girlfriends before now, but my wife was another matter. Damn, I'd take her to the mall every day if it meant that she'd leave her room.

After a half hour, Nora walked up to me and burrowed her face into my shoulder.

"I want to go home."

I kissed her temple. "We'll go home, baby."

We went on my bike, and I was glad that she'd made an effort today. I wasn't a patient man, but I knew that her post-miscarriage depression wasn't a physical problem that I could fight. If any man threatened her, he'd regret it within seconds. But her depression was harder to handle, because it was inside of her. She was both the disease and the cure, and all

I could do was wait for her to be ready.

When I was parking my bike, my phone buzzed.

"Babe, what do you want to do this afternoon?"

"I'm going to hang out on the balcony for a little — get a little sun."

"We can go to the beach."

"Another day." I got the impression that Nora was exhausted from going to the mall and pulling herself together.

I followed her upstairs, noticing the smooth swing of her ass in front of me. Damn, my wife was fine. I made a mental note to get her on her back soon. It'd been a while for us.

I remembered that my phone had buzzed. She went and sat on the balcony, and I read the text.

I felt like all the blood had drained from my face. There was ice in my veins as I read a short text that meant the end of everything.

Axed

Nora

When I got into the bedroom, Chris was flat on his back, staring sightlessly at the ceiling.

"Hello."

"Hi."

I sat at the edge of the bed.

"What's going on? Is something wrong?"

He rubbed his eyes with one hand. "Something's gone wrong."

"Yeah?"

"My co-founder Brayden quit today."

I touched his shoulder gently. "What does that mean?"

"I think my startup is done."

"Oh, no."

"That's an understatement."

"But you've worked so hard on it."

"I have. The market doesn't care about hard work. It cares about what you can sell. I've been AWOL while you've been sick. Without a technical co-founder, I'm dead in the water."

"Can't you code?"

"Barely. I know some Python and Java."

"What are you going to do?"

He rolled over so that he was facedown on the bed.

"Not sure," he said, his reply muffled by the pillow.

I looked at the tattoo peeking out from beneath his clothes. He seemed a mile away from the man I'd married in Vegas, someone in the moment, someone who took charge. I appreciated the moment, that Chris was showing his vulnerable side to me. He'd been there for me, and I could hardly do less for him.

I curled up next to him and hugged him with one arm. All I had were more questions, but he'd probably asked himself the same things over and over again.

It was the intimate moment we'd had. I saw the person inside of Chris' devil-may-care attitude.

"This matters to you, doesn't it?"

I stroked his back softly, rubbing in slow circles.

"Yes." He blew out a long breath. "I wanted to prove my dad that I'm not a fuck up. It turns out that I am."

"He doesn't think you're a fuck up."

"I normally think with my fists. Do you know how many times that he's had to send a lawyer to get me out of jail?"

"No."

"Neither do I. It can't be counted on your fingers. Or toes. Twice over."

"I never heard about all of this."

"Laila's never heard about it. It's between me and my dad. Mom and Laila never hear about it."

"But you're older now."

"I wanted my dad to think so, sure." He covered his eyes with his arm. "I don't think that I'm old enough for this. Adulthood is hard."

I kissed his muscular forearm. "You'll find a way out. It'll be fine. How much money will you lose?"

"It's not the money." Chris shrugged. "I have plenty of money. He wants me to buy back all of his stock, and I can do it. It just sucks. All we've got is an MVP and a lot of plans."

"MVP? Most valuable player like Steve Nash?"

"No. It's a minimum viable product. It's basically the least that you can get away with. We're just now seeing some adoption."

"Why is he bailing just when you guys are getting traction?"

"He's been sending pissed emails about me...being otherwise occupied."

"What's your next step?" It was funny, because I'd felt colorless and energy-less not that long ago, but I'd pull myself together to be here for Chris, to give him anything he needed today.

"I've got to talk my a lawyer."

"You want me to come with you?"

He turned to look at me. "You'd come with me?"

"Anything for you. I know that you've been holding me down, and I'd repay it five times over. I appreciate it," I said softly, pushing his hair off of his forehead. I kissed him softly on his mouth, and I watched his eyelids flutter.

I got off of the bed and pulled his legs off.

"Hey!"

"Let's get going. Get your ass in gear."

Chris came off of the bed and pulled me over his shoulder. He spanked one cheek.

"Let's shower."

We got into the shower, and he put me on my feet. He bent his head and leaned forward to kiss me breathless. Then he took shower gel and rubbed my whole body, rubbing it into my skin. I knew that I would smell like him, and I loved the idea of his essence being all over me.

I returned the favor, and we never stopped kissing, even as his fingers found their way between my thighs. He discovered the wetness between my legs, wetness that had nothing to do with the water pouring down around us.

I panted as he forced me into an orgasm. My muscles spasmed around him, and I would've fallen if he hadn't held me up.

When I opened my eyes again, I sank to my knees. Without waiting for permission or anything from him, I took him inside of my mouth. He shouted, but it faded. I used my tongue and hands to bring him to the edge of ecstasy, and I drank him down as he released inside of my warm mouth.

"Damn. We're never going to get to the lawyer if we keep going like this."

He kissed me hard, and I pushed him away a fraction of an inch.

"We've got to get dressed. I promise that we'll get naked tonight. And it'll be worth the wait."

I looked at the fire in his eyes, and I thought about taking it back.

I shook off the thought of staying in bed with him all day. We had responsibilities, and the faster we got

through the legal tangle of his co-

founder deserting him, the faster we'd

be able to focus on us and our

marriage.

Intellectual Property Lawyer

Chris

We were dressed and in my Lambo when my phone buzzed. It was a media alert; I'd set up an alert for my name and my company's name a long time ago.

I felt my breath come in fast.

"What's going on?"

Instead of answering, I gave her the phone and swerved into a parking slot.

"Your company is pivoting? That's news to me...I thought that your co-founder was abandoning..." Her voice trailed off. "Oh."

I took a quick breath, and then I got us back on the road.

We went to the nondescript building where my lawyer's office was. It was full of mahogany and gleaming edges, ensuring that we felt that we got our money's worth when we paid a high hourly rate for their expertise.

I was never as grateful that they took all the legal stuff out of my hands as when Benoit Bouvier told me the good news.

"So have I got this right? When I buy him out, I own the property?"

"Yes. He can't just leave, get the money, and then set up a startup with the same code. It's not right."

"So what are our options?"

"We're going to send over a cease-and-desist."

"Can we do that? I mean, he wrote it."

"Yes, he did, but you will have paid for it. You will own everything."

I said a silent prayer. "Okay. Let's move forward."

My lawyer nodded. "I'll get my best people on it." He looked at my hand in Nora's. "Don't worry about it. We'll figure it out."

Nora and I stood up, waved, and left.

We walked into a tiny coffeeshop called Brews and Stews. It was a very unique local coffee shop that sold soup and coffee during the winter months. During the summer months, it turned into a frozen yogurt place that let you choose your own toppings and pay per ounce.

"It's that it, then? You just pay him what he asked, and then you sue him for infringing on your intellectual property?"

"It looks like it." The day was looking brighter. I had my girl by my side, and my company had been given CPR. If we could just get my former co-founder to sell like he wanted, we'd have his balls in our grip. I couldn't wait to make him sing like a soprano.

I got an Americano from the counter, and Nora got a decaf mocha cappucino with soy milk.

We sat down in the corner, and I put my hand on her knee. We looked at each other, exchanging more in silence than we could if we spoke.

We would be okay.

Peach Ice Cream

Nora

FIVE MONTHS LATER

"Chris, I need peach ice cream."

He groaned. "I just bought you mint chocolate chip. Not even two hours ago."

"I need it."

He picked up his keys and walked to the car without another word.

I felt guilty for sending him out like this, but it was getting weird to drive with my big pregnant belly. My legs were short enough that there wasn't a lot of space between the steering wheel and my tummy on a normal day, and I had a big baby bump now. I'd gotten pregnant not long after Chris' company had reached its crisis. It turned out that stress relief could lead to a little more. I'd been scared, since I was still sliced up on the inside, but my OBGYN had given us the green light.

I heard the engine start and garage door open, and Chris' headlights lit up the front of the house before he left.

I heard the garage door close.

I went up to the nursery to look at everything. We still had all the stuff from my first pregnancy, and I hoped against hope that I would actually get to use it with this one.

I laid down in bed, putting a hand on my baby bump. The baby nudged me, and I smiled. I felt so heavy and terrible, but it was worth it when my little one bumped me. It reminded me that all this was worth it.

* * *

I dozed off, and I must've napped for a very long time. I was stiff when I woke up, and I stretched.

I checked the bedside clock, and I frowned. Chris should've been home by now.

I went to my phone and called him.

"Pick up!" I commanded him.

But all I got was voicemail.

I had a little prickling of the hairs of the back of my neck and a feeling in the pit of my stomach that something was wrong. I didn't want to jump to conclusions, so I went and checked Chris' Find My Phone.

But it was turned off entirely.

I almost bit my nails, but I stopped myself. I was sure that my husband had a good reason for not coming home yet. Maybe the first grocery store didn't have peach ice cream, and he was driving around at night looking for a 24-hour grocery store that had peach ice cream in stock.

* * *

All the stress made me tired, and I went to sleep on the couch in the living room. If — no, when — Chris came home, I'd be right there to see him.

* * *

When I woke up, cheerful sunlight was streaming through the windows. Chris hadn't come home last night.

The ball of dread that had taken root yesterday turned into a boulder. Where was he?

I called Laila.

"Hello?"

"Laila, it's Nora."

"What's up, sweetie? You sound stressed."

"Chris didn't come home last night — I'm not sure where he is."

"He's not at my house or my parents' house."

"How can you be sure?"

"I had dinner over there last night so I could tell them about the baby— trust me, I would've noticed if Chris had shown up."

I sighed quietly. "Thanks, Laila."

"No problem, sugar."

We hung up, and I paced around the kitchen. Where could Chris be?

Van

Chris

I had just gotten out of my car at the supermarket when someone parked a dark blue van right next to me. I went around their car, trying to get in and out as quickly as possible.

But I didn't expect someone to come at me with a rag soaked with chloroform.

Someone grabbed me from behind. I immediately elbowed him in the gut. I could hear him grunt in pain, but the chloroform was too hard to resist. Before I could fight him too much, I could feel my body getting limp.

I felt someone punch me in the nuts, and they exploded in white-hot agony just as I drifted into unconsciousness.

* * *

When I woke up, I was in the back of a van. I could feel that my hands were zip-tied behind my back, and I wiggled a little.

"Oh, you're awake."

I turned my head towards the voice, and I realized that the van wasn't dark. I was blindfolded.

"Who are you?"

"Someone you shouldn't have crossed."

I shifted, and I felt the echoes of agony going through my groin.

"Your nuts are bruised. You deserve it, motherfucker. In fact..." I felt a boot come down to crush my balls. I gritted my teeth to keep from crying out. They didn't deserve to hear it. I gritted my teeth even more tightly as the boot came down to hit me again. "That's for cracking my rib, bastard."

I breathed slowly, trying to contain the pain.

Where was I? I could feel that we were moving, so I figured that they were driving me somewhere.

I bitch-slapped the little kid inside of me who wanted to know where we were going and what they wanted. There was no place for fear now.

I wasn't fighting for myself here. I needed to get back to my wife and kid.

"Listen, I'll pay whatever you want. I just need to get home."

"You aren't going to be able to pay your way out of this one."

I stopped breathing. I could recognize the voice.

"Brayden?"

"That's right, motherfucker."

I felt something hard hit my face, and I lost my grip on consciousness.

* * *

When I woke up again, my hands were tied to a chair.

"Hello, Chris."

My chin came up. "Brayden."

"Didn't think that a skinny little geek could take you, huh? But you've put yourself in this position."

"Brayden, untie me. We can talk this out."

Brayden spat on my face. I couldn't wipe it away, and the spit slid down my face, dripping down my chin and into my collar.

"The time for words is over."

He casually back-handed me, and I winced. I was definitely going to have a bruise on my cheek, and he'd just hit that spot again.

And then he hit me again.

"Not nice, is it, to be cornered?"

"What are you talking about, Brayden? You're the one who left the company, not..."

He pistol-whipped me this time, and I tasted the iron of my blood as my teeth cut my cheek. I felt one get a little loose, and I tested it with my tongue. It wiggled just a little bit, as if I were a 6-year-old losing his baby teeth. I swallowed my blood and felt the thickness of it. I choked a little on my blood.

"What's this about, Brayden?"

"My investors just pulled out of my company."

"Man, that's not my business. It's yours. You left."

"You asshole. You used your father to talk to all the VCs in the area, and the people who pledged to lead my Series A have pulled out. And I've got nothing left. Nothing to lose. Nothing to gain. My company is dead in the water." He was breathing hard. "And it's all because of you. You and your stupid damn lawsuit about intellectual property. I coded this whole thing from scratch, and you just...stole it with your fancy lawyer and trust-fund money."

"I'm not the one who made that happen. You left. You wanted to make your own company with a bigger cut. It's not my fault that you didn't realize what you'd sold to me."

He grabbed a knife from his pocket and held it against my throat. The edge of the blade was cold, and I could feel it press against my throat. He cut me, just a little, and I couldn't stop the rush of fear as I bled. Just a little.

"Here's what's going to happen. You're going to call your lawyer. You're going to call this whole thing off. You're going to sign a paper and get it notarized saying that I have ownership of all of the code. And you're going to do it in the next hour, or you're going to have a hole in your head."

"Okay, yeah." As soon as I got out of here, I could call my lawyer again. No big deal.

I realized then that Brayden's pupils were dilated.

And I realized that he was worse off than I thought.

Drugs

Chris

"What are you on, Brayden?"

"On? What are you talking about?"

"What are you smoking? I can smell it."

"You can't smell shit," he shouted. He brought the knife against my throat a little harder. "You can't smell anything!"

"I can't smell anything." I agreed with the man whose knife was cutting my throat. Then I rocked my body forward, stood, and used the solid metal chair to club Brayden. It wasn't much, but it was all I had.

He was off balance, but he was reaching for the knife again. I stepped on his right hand, breaking it and his wrist, too.

I looked around for his cell phone, and I kicked him in the head. He wasn't the only one who could knock someone out.

I had no idea how many people were working with him, and I needed to get out of here pronto. I could take one person with my hands tied, but I didn't like my chances if even one more person entered the mix.

I crushed his cell phone with my boot and slowly loped towards the door. It was awkward to move with my hands tied to this chair with zip ties, and I swore to get them off as soon as I could get somewhere safe.

I got out the door, and I could see from the trees that I was in the middle of nowhere.

I needed to get somewhere where someone would find me. Right now, my only landmarks were trees.

I stumbled into the forest, making more sound than I wanted to. This chair was really cramping my style, and I didn't have the luxury of the time to cut it off of me. It was a makeshift weapon, not terribly effective, but it would work for now.

I walked towards a cave, and I took stock.

I was a little beat up — I was probably going to need to see a dentist about my loose tooth — but I knew that I was in good enough shape to make it to a road or something. I needed to find my way out of here and towards safety.

I looked for sharp rocks. There was a lot of cussing and I cut myself, but I eventually got the zip-ties off of my hands. I frankly made so much noise that I half-expected a pack of wolves to come out of the forest and eat me. But someone was smiling on me, and no wild animals came.

When I was free of the chair, I sat on it for a while to decide whether I wanted to take it. Con: It was heavy. Pro: It could be used as a club. I decided to discard it, because it was just too heavy to deal with right now.

I couldn't tell which direction I was going in. Moss grew on the north side of trees, right? So I went and marked the trees as I went, hoping that I'd be able to find a house or something. I knew that Nora had to be worried by now.

When I saw a flashlight, I knew that I wasn't out of the woods yet.

Out of the Woods

Nora

The police officer looked at me. "It's Chris."

I sank to my knees and shed a few tears. Thank goodness.

"Where is he? Is he hurt? What happened?"

"He's alive. He's in a truck heading towards the hospital. We can meet him there."

After Chris had been gone for far too long, I had called the cops. They hadn't taken me seriously, because he hadn't been missing for 24 hours. It took a phone call to Mr. King to make the wheels turn, and then pretty much the entire police force turned out to look for Chris King. When you were a billionaire, law enforcement treated you totally differently.

They'd spread out in the surrounding area, but we had no idea where he was. They found his car outside of Albertsons. It was locked, so they knew that he'd been fine when he left the car. There were a few parking lot cams that showed Chris being knocked out and thrown into a van, but we had no idea where he went from there. A dark van would be a dime a dozen, and it wasn't even that easy to check things out at night.

But when Hudson King asks you to look for his missing son, you don't half-ass it.

I got into the squad car and headed for the hospital. It was handy that we got to use the wailing lights, although I held my hands over my ears during the ride.

We were at the hospital in 15 minutes, and I was out of the car before the police officer even fully parked. I ran into the hospital.

"Excuse me," I told the front desk receptionist, "I'm here to see Chris King."

"And you are?"

"His wife."

She blinked at me. "You're real young."

"I am."

She shrugged. "Okay. He's in room 218. I can have someone guide you there." A volunteer wearing a red polo came out from behind the desk, and I walked up to Chris' room.

Something inside of me relaxed when I saw Chris in that bed. He was wired to a bunch of things that beeped, and he had an IV stuck into him, but he was there.

Alive.

I rushed to him.

"Hey, babe."

Even in bed, Chris was a super flirt. He flicked his eyes over me and told me, "Looking good."

I cried a little bit as I hugged him, careful of his IV. "Don't disappear again. I don't think that my heart can take it."

"I think that I can promise that."

"What happened? I thought that my heart stopped when we saw someone stuff you inside of a van."

"It was Brayden."

I stilled. "Brayden? Your former co-founder Brayden?"

"His company fell apart." Chris shrugged as much as he could. "And he wanted to take it out on someone, so he chose me."

I was filled with anger. "And what'll happen to him?"

"I sent the police back to find him. They found him unconscious in the cabin where he held me. He'll go away for a long time."

"Who would think that the two of us would be kidnapped in such a short time period?"

"I think I've had all the kidnapping I can stand in a lifetime, Nora."

I leaned in and kissed him. I heard his heart rate pick up a little bit...and then it picked up a lot.

"Let's make a pact never to get kidnapped again, okay?"

"It's a deal."

Chris' eyes closed, and I put my free hand on my tummy. The three of us were a little family, and we were

safe and sound again.

Epilogue

"It's a girl!"

I felt my heart fill with pride as the slimy baby was picked up by the doctor. We hadn't wanted to know the gender before the baby was born. We just kept all the stuff that we'd bought for the first baby. We were well-equipped to bring this little life into the world.

The nurses and doctors whisked our little girl off to be washed, measured, and pinched. I heard her crying as they spanked the baby, and it was a good sound. Her lungs were just fine.

I went to stand by my sweaty wife. She had never been more beautiful to me.

"We're never having another one," she croaked. "You're never getting another baby."

"That's what they all say," the obstetric nurse told us. "But it's funny — when you fall in love with your first, it's hard to resist making a second one."

Nora shook her head. "You're going to get snipped," she commanded. "I'm never going through labor again."

I kissed her hand, the hand that had squeezed all the blood out of mine while she had gone through agonizing hours of labor.

"I love you," I told her. We would hash out the rest later.

"I love you, too."

THE END

www.ingramcontent.com/pod-product-compliance
Lightning Source LLC
Chambersburg PA
CBHW060520260626
47161CB00003B/710